Storm of Ascension

Storm of Ascension

C.H. Williams

ISBN- 13: 978-1-7333569-3-0

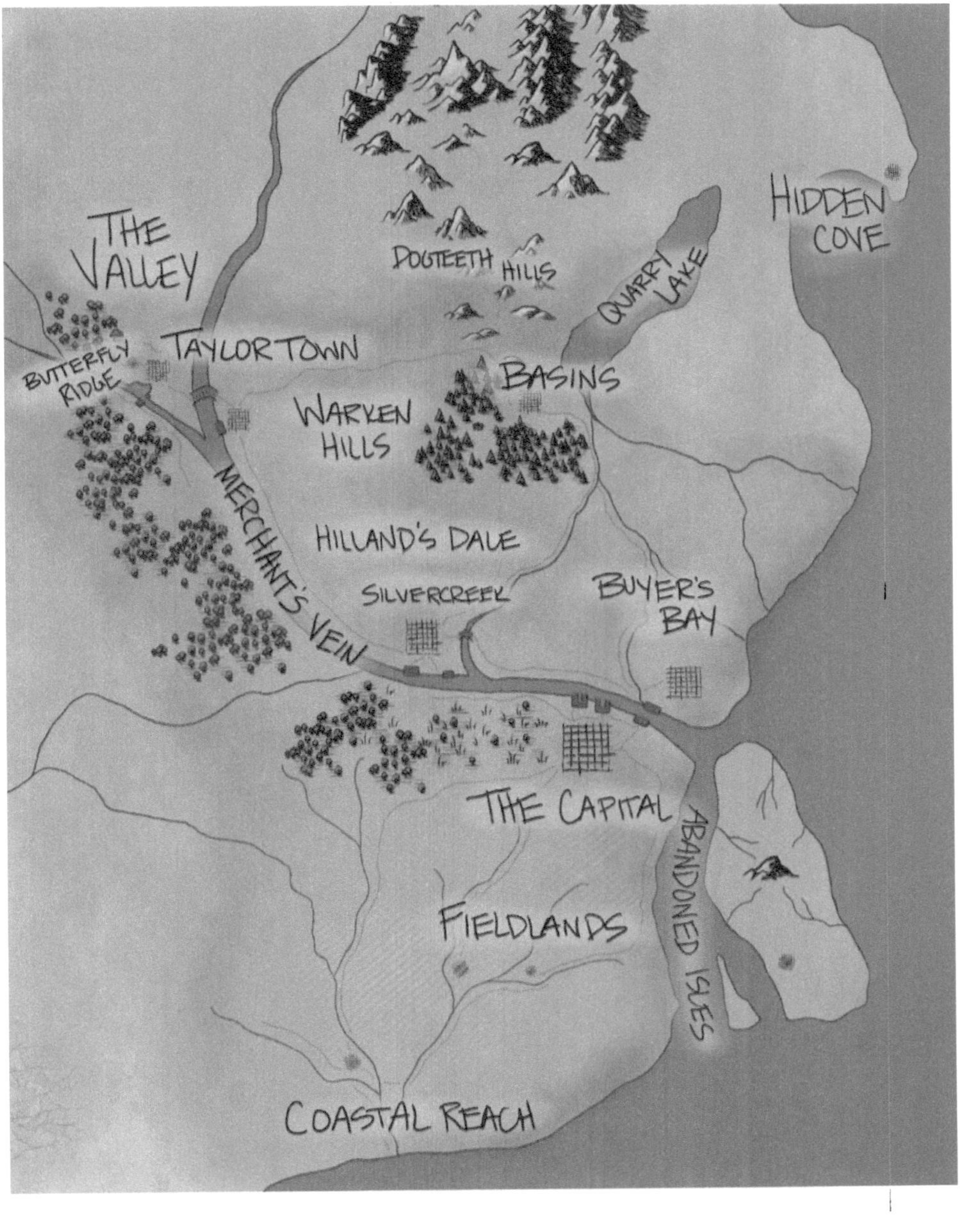

THE VALLEY
DOGTEETH HILLS
QUARRY LAKE
HIDDEN COVE
BUTTERFLY RIDGE
TAYLORTOWN
BASINS
WARKEN HILLS
MERCHANT'S VEIN
HILLAND'S DALE
SILVERCREEK
BUYER'S BAY
THE CAPITAL
ABANDONED ISLES
FIELDLANDS
COASTAL REACH

PROLOGUE

A few months ago, Commissioner Foster relinquished his role as head of the Capital District, taking his fortunes and his three children, Grayson, Juli, and Lilah, north to seek their fortunes in the Wilderness.

He left behind utter chaos.

Confidence in the Guild has weakened with his departure, and with rumors of other Commissioners looking to flee, our stability has been compromised.

The smaller districts, like ours, the Coastal Reach, are being looked to for support.

I fear what we can deliver may not be enough, for even if we should step up, I wonder how it will be that Aerdela withstands the coming storm.

EXCERPT FROM THE DIARY OF COMMISSIONER ADA FOLLEREY

Chapter 1

ADA

"COMMISSIONER FOSTER HAS DEPARTED, TAKING HIS THREE BRATS with him, and where does that leave me? Fucked, that's where!" Owin paused for a long moment, then slammed his hand on the table for emphasis, the delay in gesture rather undermining the intensity he'd perhaps been aiming for. "And you know what's out there, in the Wild. Monsters and—and *magic,* and all sorts of wretched things! Curses, a-a-a-and shadows—"

Ada fixed her gaze on Owin from where she lingered in the balcony above the Guild chambers, face blazing with shame.

She loved her father, but a scene the likes of which he loved to make wouldn't do well to cement his authority in the wake of the exodus.

Another merchant scoffed, rolling their eyes. "Simply because you have made a string of bad investments—"

"The investments wouldn't have gone *bad* if Foster had remained at his post, instead of departing post-haste on some half-cocked mission to expand the empire!"

The arguments had been raging for weeks.

The Guild was a finely oiled machine, working perfectly within the confines of their borders. Until someone grew restless, and started saying poetic nonsense like *there's a grand old world out there, chaps,* and *what might lie ahead could be unimaginable, my dear fellow,* and then everyone was packing up their bags and heading out.

"We have the opportunity for the first time since the war to grow—"

"They are leaving the coast in droves!" Owin shrieked, face purple. "Factories are shutting down hither and yon, the first taste of economic stability we've had in a hundred years, gone, and the rumors at the borders, you should hear what kinds of awful things are encroaching, all because Foster has made us a vulnerable target, you cannot imagine the creatures—it's dark sorcery at work, I am telling you—"

"Ow!" Ada whispered, unclenching her fist from the ornament at the center of her ribboned belt. Resting her hands about her waist, as did the other ladies of the gallery, she'd been fidgeting with the bejeweled starburst sun, until at last she simply taken to gripping it tight in her fist.

Until now, that was. The slice along her hand welled with blood, a thick drop splattering to the stone floor.

I wish we could truly forget the curses and shadows and gods-damned magic of our great-grandparent's war, she thought bitterly, pulling her handkerchief from the skirt pocket to stem the flow.

Ada couldn't linger any longer.

Turning, she left the other listeners watching the ungodly display.

Owin Follerey was a kind man. He was a wary businessman, skeptical to the point of snapping, and considered by all to be a passionate person. They were admirable traits, when considered generally, but during the Guild assemblies, they were nothing short of disastrous.

The streets of the Capital were cold and empty and unfamiliar as Ada pushed past the guards of the Guild chambers, abandoning the stuffy building for the chill of winter beyond. Departing before the session's end was a temporary luxury, though—next year, it would be Ada, standing in her father's place.

And what will you say, when they ask about the strange things happening at the district borders.

Will you deny it?

Will you deny that we are naive, ignoring something we do not understand?

Something wretched and fantastical had already ripped their world apart once.

Shattered families. Blood-soaked earth. This was the legacy of Ada's forebearers. Peaceful secrets. A bit of hope. This would be Ada's.

She shuddered, a reaction that she told herself had nothing to do with the impending mantel she was to carry, and everything to do with the cold winds whipping the Capital.

It would be warmer at home in the Coastal Reaches, she thought bitterly. But at least the burgeoning winter further north gave her leave to don the plaid and pleated woolen skirts and lacy, high-collared blouses of the Capital women. A small grace.

They'd let a house a few blocks from the chambers, as they did every winter, when the Commissioners gathered in a quasi-tribunal to hear the issues that had accumulated through the rest of the year and discuss matters of state.

But this winter was different, Ada thought, a small smile tugging at her lips as she watched the skirt with delight, hem kissing the cobblestones as she stepped off the curb to cross the street.

Her last winter as an attache to her father, as an observer to the politics

Her smile faltered. Ada had been poised to ascend with another, too. Her father's health was failing, and she'd been supposed to step up the same year Grayson Foster did, the son of the same Commissioner Foster that Ada's father so viciously and rightfully attacked five minutes ago in the Guild Chambers.

She missed Grayson. And Juli, too, and Lilah.

Seasonal friends, they'd all been, with the ventures to the Capital bringing them all together once again with the changing of seasons.

One day.

Their journeys had overlapped by one stinking day, and it was hardly enough to say goodbye.

I am so happy for you, Grayson had whispered into her ear, giving her a tight older-brother hug. *Ada, this is wonderful. Congratulations.*

Juli's eyes had been brimming with tears as she'd pressed her hands into Ada's. *I can't believe we have to go. You're my sister, though, as much as Lilah, please remember that?*

Lilah had given Juli a derisive glare, evidence of the ever-fierce battle raging continually between them, but it'd melted as she'd turned to Ada. *You are radiant,* she'd said softly. *Please write, Ada? I simply can't imagine not hearing about all the wonderful things you're going to keep doing.*

And with that, it'd been goodbye.

At least it hadn't been Emerly, leaving.

The Fosters—they were sweet, to be sure, but it'd been Emerly who'd been there, when it mattered.

Emerly, too, who was waiting upstairs, Ada thought, apprehension from her father's disgusting display starting to dissipate as she made her way up the front walk of the brick facade house on the corner. Emerly, because Ada hadn't been able to face the Capital alone.

Not this time.

Not in the shadow of her ascension.

Chapter 2

EMERLY

EMERLY stood, arms crossed, watching ADA in the street below.

The way the hem of her dress gathered up the dying leaves, only to abandon them once more as she stepped up onto the sidewalk, skirt brushing the curb with an easy sigh.

The way she looked askance into the windowpane of the neighboring house, not trying to spare a glance inside, but rather, trying to catch her reflection in the dark.

He'd known her for as long as he could remember.

The Coastal Reach had been a lush canvas for imaginative children, and they'd spent their days running through the orchards, stealing under-ripe peaches from trees, or else playing in the warm turquoise waters that lapped against the southern shore.

Adolescence had found them both angsty and irate, unraveling the complexities life offered them. Their secluded life in the Coastal Reach had proved a sweet refuge, but the real world was fast-encroaching, and it had hit them both with heartache, albeit of different sorts. Ada had found, at the hands of others, hurt and disappointment, and questions, questions like *why do I not feel at home in my own skin* and later, *why do I feel less like a son and so much more like a daughter.* Emerly—he had been born deaf, just like his mother. Their close-knit community that welcomed the deaf was one thing, but taking to the world had been another, and those who did not sign simply did not care to understand what it meant, to be different.

Then, there'd been everything that'd happened in the spring.

This spring had brought so much change. Good change, unquestionably. Change all the same, though, and Ada had been in tears as they sat talking by the firelight.

They'd been raised together, their families close to inseparable, and so Emerly and Ada had spent many a late night, signing back and forth in the dancing light, and this night had seemed like no other, until her eyes started to glisten, and she'd told him.

I want you to call me Ada.

Watching her move up the walk, he sighed, sinking back down into his place in the window seat, drawing his book close. He knew her routine.

She'd spent the morning in the Guild Chambers; the moment she'd walk through the door, she'd inquire about the mail, hoping for a letter from Sebastian. She'd written to him, and it was odd, that he hadn't written back. They corresponded regularly, happily calling each other dear friends—until he'd simply stopped writing back.

We will find him, she'd said, a worried look on her face as they'd bumped along in the carriage, making the annual journey into the Capital. *If he's not at the docks, then we'll go the Island itself.*

Just a short way off the eastern coast lay the Abandoned Island. Home to those who eschewed the Guild, it thrived, poised between past and present. Emerly's father had a friend from the Island, a salty man with brilliant red hair and piercing green eyes—a metalsmith, whose talent for hooks his father always boasted about...

Emerly bid the thoughts away.

They only served to make him homesick for the Coastal Reach.

This had been the first year he'd accompanied Ada to the Capital on her family's pseudo-pilgrimage, and choosing between missing his home and missing Ada, it had been no contest.

He'd be at her side until the end.

Chapter 3

SEBASTIAN

THE RUINS OF THE CITADEL STOOD TALL, SHADOWS CRAWLING LONG across the crumbling road.

"I love this place," Sebastian whispered. "I spent my life, wandering through these ruins. Part of me will always belong to the Citadel, I think."

The hermit snorted. "That *is* the requirement, boy. If you wish to get something in return, you must be willing to make the sacrifice." Knifepoint ears sliced up, ears of the *vora*, of elves that lived in memory.

Sebastian could feel the magic, heavy and old, lingering beneath his feet as he gazed across the wreckage of the Citadel. Once the pinnacle of human learning, it had decayed, now nothing more than a forgotten relic.

And this place...

What was once a great empire was now nothing beyond a small fishing village, forgotten by all but a few whose memory ran old, and the ones who themselves had remained on the island.

His warmed-earth skin was set into relief as he stooped down, letting his fingers run through the ashen sand. "All I have to do is make a blood-pact, and I can be with Lee?"

Lee was everything to him.

Lee, and her fins and scales and tail. Lee was a kind of undine, he was given to understand. *Merfolk,* his grandma called them, and in fact, Lee should've been impossible, but he'd learned, in his nineteen years on the island that too much of what shouldn't have been was, and that the memory of the island was not that of their Guilded counterparts.

They'd been courted time and again by the Guild.

But the island remained a conglomeration of those who'd stayed behind, after the war, who wished above all else, to be forgotten.

And forgotten they would be.

He would sink their forgotten Citadel beneath the waves, a sacrifice to the magic below. And beneath the waves, he too would go.

"You will spill your blood onto the sand," the hermit crooned. "Life is in the blood, boy. And with Life, Death, too. They walk hand-in-hand, child, bitter rivals and bonded brethren. Slit your palm, make the pact with the earth, and we shall invoke the magic that governs the gods themselves. Magic not even the gods could master."

What it would've been like, to see this place in its heyday, when those very gods the hermit spoke of walked the streets, and magic ran free.

His letter from Ada was crumpled in his pocket.

He couldn't bear to write her back.

To tell her he wouldn't going to the Capital this year, with the rest of the fishermen, to sell their wares for a tidy sum when the Merchants came calling.

He'd had the note drafted for almost a month before her letter had come, and now...

It would break her heart.

As it broke his.

Dear Ada, it would have to say. *I am sorry, I'm not coming back. I have decided to seek my fortune with the sea.*

Beneath the sea, more like.

It had felt like an impossible choice, and it was a trade he told himself he would have never made, if there'd been any other choice.

But there was no other option.

No path forward but to make the sacrifice, and live beneath the waves.

Sebastian, he could hear Ada saying, exasperated. *Why? It's heartache. It will fade.*

But it wouldn't.

"You can make me like Lee," Sebastian asked, glancing up at the hermit from where he knelt on the sand. "You can make me undine, too, like you did to her? If I make the blood-pact, and give the ruins to the ocean, I can be like her?"

"You're not a dreamer." The hermit frowned, crouching down beside Sebastian. Then, raising an eyebrow, he gave Sebastian's pocket a prod, where Ada's letter sat inside. "Your friend? She's a dreamer."

"How did you—"

"I know. They're the dreamers, and I was their servant." He flicked a pebble, sending it flying. Then, rising, he crooked an old finger at Sebastian, beckoning him to follow. "Come. It is time. Tonight, we make the blood-pact. And tomorrow, the island will fall."

Chapter 4

LEE

THE WATER WAS TEPID AGAINST HER SKIN AS LEE DRIFTED, watching the waves distort the gray sky above.

Sebastian was being ridiculous.

Sebastian.

She let his name wash over her, *Sebastian, Sea-bash-chen, seab-ash, ash, Sebastian* and his name was like waves.

Sink the Citadel.

He would never.

It was not the romantic sunken city of his novels, nor a passage from the stories he read to her on the beach when the days were warm and the wind was gentle. There would be no cathedral bells tolling in grandeur beneath the waves.

If he managed to bring the ruins to meet the sea...

She gave a shudder, and in a smooth roll, turned for the ocean floor below.

Many had wished to dance beneath the sea.

Many bloated corpses had washed up upon the shore.

The undine were a myth brought to life, in her, and her alone.

Weary travelers saw undine in the spray of waterfalls and in turbulent rivers, in the depths of lakes and in the distant ocean crashing on the shore, but the tired mind could conjure up any sort of trick, and anyway, the god of Death wasn't so much in the business of soul-bargains.

Lee knew this, for a fact, for she'd come face-to-face with Death herself.

I don't make bargains. But I will make an exception for you, child, Death had grinned, standing on the shores of the beyond. *After all, you loved the sea to death, did you not?*

Lee had.

She'd loved the sea, loved the way the waves seemed to whisper their secrets to her, the salt water against her cheeks the softest kisses, and Lee should not have been out swimming, that day, but she went, and she drowned, and she met the Ender of Stories, the Cutter of Threads, the Rival of Life, the one who harbored souls in the waystation of the Underworld until they were ferried across the river to the Beyond.

Death, who held her soul as collateral, so Lee could swim a little longer.

Maybe it'd been a favor to the daughter of a family who carried on the legacy of Death from their home hidden up the rocky coast, a city of unimaginable magic. If it had been, though, it wasn't much of one. It'd seemed like such a gift, to the drowned girl who didn't want to die. Her soul, in exchange for a while longer amongst the living.

Anymore, though, it felt like a curse.

A lonely, miserable curse.

You do not understand, Lee had snapped, watching Sebastian recoil at her words. *You do not know how much would have to be given, to be like me.* He did not fully understand what it meant, to live adrift from kin. Did not fully realize that her life was the joke of a twisted god, that she had drowned and been resurrected for the sake of a good laugh from an immortal.

And you do? he'd countered. *Tell me, L, when did having magic in your veins make you the unequivocal expert in practice?*

I might ask the same of you, she'd snarled. *When did being in love mean you've lost all sense of reason?*

He'd stormed off, and she'd dived beneath the waves.

She could not change what had happened.

She could not change that those above went about their lives, walking on their own two feet, could not change that beneath the water lived a girl, alone, made and left at the hands of a hermit and a god, could not change that Sebastian was a boy who savored the salt water against his skin, could not change that he loved to spend his summer days in the waves, could not change that she'd been drifting along, watching the clouds, and he'd seen her.

She could not change that she loved him deeply.

And their lives would be spent trading hours on the rocky isle, where he could sit on the shore and she could lilt half-hidden in the waves, until it was time to say goodbye.

Night always fell fast, under the sea.

She'd drifted up one last time, breathing in the cold night air, before retreating to a bed of seaweed and sand in the flooded caverns.

Usually, sleep found her with ease.

Not tonight.

A glimmer of distorted moon had tumbled down, cutting through the water, falling coolly on the bluish-green scales, onto the webbed fins. Her pinkish skin had left the wan complexion of the sea behind, with

Sebastian. So much time in the sun, up above.

And in the night, in the sleepless night, she played a game.

What if he were here.

What if I were there.

What if we could hold each other through the dark.

The thoughts only brought tears.

From the ocean, the stinging salt, she thought bitterly. And to the ocean, the salt water returns.

Such is the way of things, in the deep.

Chapter 5

ADA

"DID THE POST COME IN YET?" ADA CALLED DOWN THE HALL, trading the stiff jacket for a wrap hanging over a hook by the door.

No reply.

Meaning that the housekeep wasn't back yet.

Meaning the post *might* have come in, only Gretta hadn't brought it back to the house just yet.

Which meant there was waiting to be done.

Waiting, and stewing, over her father's abysmal display.

She found Emerly in his room, which adjoined hers via a door her parents were reasonably sure was locked but most certainly wasn't, and that suited both her and Emerly just fine.

They'd been inseparable, of late.

Sitting in the window seat, book in his lap, he glanced up, blonde hair mussed. A smile split across his face, his fingers leaving the pages to move deftly through the air, a silent question written with his hands. "You're back early," he noted.

She sighed, only bothering to send up a rude gesture in the direction of the Guild chambers.

But Emerly seemed to appreciate it, chuckling quietly as he patted the seat next to him, tossing the book gently to the floor. "Come. Sit."

Sinking down, she was deeply aware of how small the window seat was.

How close they were, sitting there, half-pressed against the cold panes, Emerly's hand on her shoulder, giving it a small squeeze to welcome her back.

She meant to meet his eyes. To give him a small smile.

Instead, Ada turned, finding her reflection in the glass.

A compulsion, of late.

"It's too short," she breathed, tossing the words into the air with her hands before moving to fuss over her hair. Growing slowly, it'd edged towards her jawline, barely enough to set in curling papers overnight, the way her mother did.

But Ada was impatient.

She craved the curls of the Capital girls, tumbling brilliantly down her back towards her waist.

Emerly clicked his tongue in dismay. "It's lovely. And it'll grow," he gestured back.

Lovely.

Ada ground her teeth, willing herself not to go red.

It didn't work.

She reflexively ran the back of her hand slowly along her jawline, eyes flitting to the ground.

Emerly caught her hand, though, stopping what would be an obsessive study of her cheeks. He gave her fingers a squeeze, resting them on his knee. "Stop. You'll wear your skin raw, at this rate. You're *fine.*"

Regretfully, she took her hand back to meet the air once more. "It doesn't feel fine."

"I know," he nodded. "Gretta said soon, though, right?"

"Yeah. Soon."

Gretta, and her wild remedies.

This time, it'd been a paste of southern herbs. *You'll have cheeks like a baby's bottom in no time, dearie, no time at all.*

No time at all had been two weeks ago, and still, Ada was waiting.

"It is a journey," Emerly gestured, hands imitating bobbing ocean waves, the signal of adventure. She loved the way it looked when he signed. Loved his hands, too, loved the hairs brushed up the back of his hand, the way the veins flared in moments of tension, and he was right, it *was* an adventure. "That's what you told me," he nodded, going on, "and besides. You're young. It's not like you were even able to grow a full—"

Ada brushed his hands aside, glaring. "Stop it."

Emerly only shrugged, finishing the thought with nothing more than a pointed look and a raised eyebrow.

In spite of herself, she felt a small smile tugging at the corners of her mouth.

He wasn't wrong.

"What happened to your hand," Emerly signed, eyes narrowing as he nodded to the red gash on her palm.

"I cut it on my belt. Nobody tells you how dangerous those things are."

"Did you put ointment on it?"

"Yes," she lied.

He pursed his lips, raising an eyebrow in skepticism. But he didn't push it further.

"Come here." He drew her in, letting her head lean against his shoulder as he pulled her into a hug.

Then, gently, he took the hand she'd sliced open, cradling it in his.

Neither would talk about what he could do. That when she stood up, there'd be no cut on her hand, nothing beyond a worried red line bearing the healing of a week or more, all in the matter of a few moments.

Nobody in the Capital would've dared, and even in the Coastal Reach, it was the kind of thing their hands would sign before the darkening fire in the dead of night.

Then again, she supposed it didn't matter.

Words, of late, had been falling flat between them for a deeper kind of language.

The kind of language that blurred lines.

That somehow reassured her and set her in unease, all at once.

"Bertie—shit, sorry—*Ada!*"

Her mother's voice from downstairs broke the moment, and Ada pulled away, giving Emerly a knowing look.

Her mother tried.

It was a change, for all of them, a change of habit that ran seventeen years deep.

"Your mother?" Emerly guessed. He'd been born unhearing, a few miles down the coast from Ada's family, a handful of months before Ada herself had met the world, and like anyone she keep close to her heart he'd learned to read her expressions with unnerving accuracy.

As much time as they'd spent together, though, how could he not.

"She used the wrong name again," Ada signed, half-heartedly rising. "She's trying, she really is..."

Emerly pursed his lips in sympathy, nodding.

Maybe her mother was well-intentioned. But Emerly knew, better than anyone, how the misstep had cut Ada to the quick.

"Hurry back," he said, catching her eyes before she turned to go. "I want to know all about the chamber meeting."

Ada brought her hand to her heart, circling it with her fingers, the signal of a pact.

I promise.

Chapter 6

EMERLY

In Ada's absence, Emerly didn't bother to return to the book he'd been pretending to read.

Instead, he turned his thoughts to their future.

Because it had to be theirs, didn't it? His, and Ada's?

And what is it you do, m'boy, someone had asked, realizing him to be a new addition to the Follerey entourage.

The proper answer was likely *aide* or *advisor,* but those felt like dishonest answers, and he'd been struck, really, by how much of propriety seemed to be a lie. If they wished to know why he was in the Capital—well, Ada had not wished to make the journey alone, and he did not wish to be parted from her. If they wished to know his vocation—he would tend to the sick, like his father.

It wasn't really talked about, anymore.

They'd strung up folks with strange talents, in the childhood of his great-grandparents. It was the kind of thing everyone knew but nobody really talked about, except in the dark of night, around a hushed dinner table, little ones paying close attention but doing their best to shrink into the shadows, lest they be remembered and sent to bed.

People had been so scared, he remembered his mother saying. Any whisper of magic—and that was it.

Of course, it was all superstition, his father had clarified, glancing around the table to see the nods of agreement from the uncles and cousins. A little idea had sparked a wildfire, and it was easier to blame misfortune on a disliked neighbor than the will of the powers that be.

And anymore, it was easier for Emerly, and everyone else, to believe he'd simply learned the talent from his father.

Easier than wondering if he'd been born to healing.

And so, he lingered, turning his gaze to the window beyond.

Clouds were swelling in the east, shadowed and angry, and Emerly leaned his head against the cool pane of glass, watching the storm brewing.

Chapter 7

SEBASTIAN

That evening found Sebastian's thoughts heavy and his palm stinging with the remnants of the pact.

Rumors about the hermit flew like flies in the heat of a summer fish market, rumors with words like *magic* and *shadows* and *the things that man can do, Sebastian, it's terrifying.*

The hermit's grotto had been dank and desperate, a fire sputtering out amid the *drip drip drip* of water from the cavern ceiling and blood from Sebastian's hand against the stone.

With this blood, I invoke the change, he'd breathed, watching the hermit sprinkle salt water atop the drops of dark, dark blood. He'd found the words in one of the crumbling scrolls of the Citadel. *I have given my blood. And in my blood, a new life.*

A promise, the blood was.

It was the old way, to seal a pact in blood.

Of course, that hadn't stopped his best friend Ernst from doing the same when they'd been younger, thinking it was funny to prick his tanned fingertip and let a single drop fall into the sand. *My word,* he'd say solemnly, watching Sebastian scoff.

To Ernst, it had been a joke.

To Sebastian, standing in the hermit's grotto as the light faded, drawing the blade across his palm, it was no such thing.

He promised the ruin of an empire, to give the old magic the crumbling stone buildings brimming with memories of the long-forgotten wars, the sieges waged in the yester-years, the battles won and lost as the stained-glass gods themselves watched from the now-crumbling Citadel towers.

In exchange for helping to bring the jutting little peninsula down into the ocean, Sebastian would sink into the sea, too.

He didn't really think about the people that would probably get hurt.

It was a horrendous part of life, living in such desperate pain that one could not fathom any price too high just for a bit of relief.

Sebastian had found it difficult, of late, to pull himself out of bed. The effort seemed to sink a new kind of exhaustion over him, each day bringing a new low he hadn't thought possible the day before.

In the grotto that afternoon, the hermit had crouched over the fire, the dim light making his pale skin wax orange before the flames. *I can read the earth,* he'd crooned, drawing lines in the sand. But the walls of stone had begun to shake, and the hermit's eyes had rolled back in his head as he breathed the words. *It is angry. Full of fury. They dream it to flames, and in flames it will break. Another crack through our world, shattered by nightmare.*

The beast below the waves was due its pay, the hermit had said.

And then I will be undine? Sebastian had asked, worried. *Then I will be like Lee?*

Only to the dreamers, I give the ladder, the hermit had chuckled again.

The hermit said that Ada was a dreamer, because being a dreamer meant she had clarity of sight, and she'd seen who she was, clearly enough. She saw that she was Ada Follerey, daughter of the Coastal Reach.

She'd been in his thoughts since her letter, but in truth, she was living in peace across the straight and it was hard to spare her worry when she'd found such happiness.

Please, her letter had practically beamed, *call me sister. Call me Ada.*

They'd met the first time he'd gone with his father to the Capital to sell their fares of winteroyster on the docks, a delicacy to the Mainland. Caught on the north-eastern edge of the island, and then, only a few months out of the year.

Of course, Ada'd been hardly an adolescent, then.

It broke his heart, that there wasn't time to take a schooner to the Mainland to see her. But with his father and sister away at sea, even if he'd wanted to, there was no way to get back. Not unless he wanted to wait until next week, when the supply ship came in, and by then, it'd be too late.

I am free, Sebastian. I am terrified and unsure of what this means, but I am free.

That was what she'd written.

She was just beginning.

But Sebastian—there was no life for him, here.

He loved the sea. Loved the feel of the slick wooden boards of the schooner beneath his feet, the salty wind on his cheeks, the blur of waves as the keel of the boat cut through the whitecaps, how it felt to tug his shirt off and dive into the cool water, to hold his breath and feel that sweet pressure hugging in tight—

And then there was Lee.

It didn't make sense.

He was a rational boy, someone with his feet on the ground, and she'd swept him away in the blink of an eye.

She was sharp.

She could tear away pretenses.

And more than anything, she made him realize how fucking enormous the world was.

As a young child, he'd worshiped the ancient ruins around their homes. Still did, he supposed. Worshipped the battle waged hundreds of years before beneath his feet. He'd played swords with his sister, pretending to slay the *vora,* living in another world, and anymore, Lee *was* that other world.

But no longer was it a world of dead saints and reborn gods.

It was tangible.

 Real.

Anything he might dream up, mind drifting as he dredged up the massive crustaceans from the ocean floor, anything he could imagine—it was his, for the taking.

Chapter 8

LEE

The night found Lee alone.

Well.

Any time of day, save her moments with Sebastian, found her alone.

Maybe at first, he believed she'd been in good company, finding people like her beneath the water.

A true fairy tale, she smirked, rising to break the surface.

It'd been a life beneath the waves, or no life at all.

A rip tide had carried her far beyond the shore of her secret little city, and as water filled her lungs, she knew it was Death she'd meet.

Her last moments of consciousness had condemned her, because she'd thought it was a funny way to die.

She'd loved the ocean.

Loved it to death.

Death thought this a funny quip, for Lee remembered meeting her at the gate, a coy smile on her lips. *You loved it to death,* she'd snickered. *Very well. Love it to death you will.*

Lee had awoken, coughing up salt water on the shore of the Citadel, a hermit peering into her eyes, and he'd given her a tail for her legs. Her soul, however, was held with Death herself.

We'll let you swim, swim, swim, he'd murmured, dragging her through the sand. *Swim, child, and be free. But you come back, and she'll be waiting on these shores.*

A cruel joke.

A curse, maybe.

That Lee would love the ocean to death.

It was hard to blame a god, though, for the work of a gods-damned *vora.*

And that's what the hermit was.

Sebastian said he'd been exiled, and she'd quipped back that of course he'd been exiled, if he'd been turning folks in to fish on top of a land-locked mountain.

That was exile-able shit, right there.

Poor planning, and poor execution.

Best send that boy to the sea, Lee said, and Sebastian had been rolling with laughter.

That he thought he was going to join her in a life of death and exile, though—now *that* was fucking hilarious.

"Sebastian," she said cautiously, peering around the boulder, arms cradling the freezing rock, squinting as buckets of lamplight broke the dark.

Pebbles slipping under foot preceded him, and he greeted her with a slight nod, a solemn look on his face. Bundled in a waxed canvas coat, the scruffy wool sweater peeking out at the collar, he looked exhausted. "Lee."

Scoffing, her shoulders sank. "Really? That's it?"

He met her gaze for a long moment.

Then, with a sigh, he stooped down, fingers brushing across her cheek before giving her a lingering kiss.

A life beneath the waves with him.

It wouldn't be the worst.

But it wasn't worth his life, and the chance that the humor of Death and her crony on the shore wouldn't last.

"I don't know why you're upset," Sebastian breathed, pulling back, eyes cold. "I am doing this for you. For us. So neither of us have to be alone."

"You are risking your life—"

"There's other ways. He said it's about balance—another sacrifice—"

"You are talking about bringing that gods-damned strip of rock into the ocean, as if muddying the waters is the same as trading your soul!"

"And maybe it is, Lee!" He glared, taking a step back. "I love the Citadel. This place is in my blood. And I am willing to wash my childhood dreams into the sea. You don't think there's magic in that? In the fact that a few days will bring another quake, another eruption, and this time, I will watch the grounds of my boyhood fantasies fall away? You think that isn't the same as trading my soul away?"

"Then what? When you've watched who you are sink away into the water, what then, Sebastian?"

He ground his teeth, sinking down onto his usual rock. "Then? Freedom, Lee. Freedom."

Chapter 9

ADA

"Dad's sure that this is the beginning of the end," Ada gushed, fingers clumsy with cold as she tried to rush through the words.

Sitting cross-legged on her bed across from Emerly, her eyes flicked to the candle burning low on her nightstand.

Hurry.

"Between the rumors of what's going on beyond Aerdela, and the Commissioner of the Capital leaving, Father has threatened to withdraw from the Guild. But all our accounts are tied up in the Foster's trade deals, which are in flux until a new Commissioner is finalized, so if we withdraw, we'll be in the same place as the Fosters. Broke. Done for."

Emerly's eyes were dark in the low light, brow knit in concentration as he watched her fingers move, nodding as he watched.

"What can I do," he said at last, meeting her eyes.

She only shook her head. "I don't know. The answer is...is right there. So close, I can almost taste it."

The candle flickered, a warning that time was running out.

And yet, Emerly was still, eyes never leaving her.

"What," she asked, movement small.

"I am glad," he answered slowly. "Glad to be here with you. In the Capital." He spared a quick glance to the open door between their rooms before his eyes flicked back to her.

"I know," she whispered, not bothering to bring her hands to speak the words. "Me, too."

He found her hands, giving them a squeeze.

And then, leaning in, he brushed a gentle kiss against her lips.

"Emerly—"

He left her hands. "A, I think you're afraid. And..." He paused. "And that's okay. I understand. But I like you back, you know."

Tears were threatening behind Ada's eyes.

She hadn't realized how close they'd come to sit, how their legs were touching, how even how, his hand was on her knee, rubbing soothing circles.

"Talk to me, Ada."

"I just—I don't know." Her eyes flicked to the candle once more, burning dangerously low. "What does that make us, Em?"

"A boy and a girl who have been in love for a long time." He shrugged. "I dunno, A. You're my best friend. And I think we've been sweet on each other for a while, now."

She nodded, wiping the tears from her cheeks. "I am," she clarified. "Sweet on you, that is."

"But?"

The candle was almost done.

They were running out of time.

"Ada, stop looking at the candle. If it burns out, we'll light another. I've got a drawer full, because I spend every night sitting on your bed, talking with *you.* Don't even have to go downstairs."

"I worry. In spite of everything we've been through, Em, there is this fear, in the back of my mind," she pressed, words flying fast, now. "What if. What if it isn't real."

"Ada." He caught her hands, a small smile on his lips as he kissed them, bringing them to rest on his legs. "A, I like you. I like you for the girl you are. You're a witty, intelligent, gorgeous woman with her head on straight and a keen sense for politics, and I love you for all of that, Ada. I know you feel like you're in flux, right now. But I am sitting here, right now, as a boy, telling you, a girl, how deeply I care for you. You're not alone."

Ada's heart was racing, temples pounding.

A thousand worries.

There were a thousand worries, and not enough time in the universe to air them all.

"Ask me the question." Ada's fingers moved through the air, a familiar command. "Do I look like a girl, to you? Right now? In this moment?"

"Do you feel like a girl?" The reply that demanded the answer come from her, and her alone.

She nodded.

Never would it be said that she let anyone else tell her who she was.

"Then you look like a girl." Emerly was smiling brightly as he signed the words. "Ada, your heart is what keeps you living. It's too important to be ignored."

With the waves of reassurance.

"And tonight," she pressed on, a sweet tightness in her chest. "Tonight, if we..."

Emerly's eyes were glistening as he nodded, beaming. "If I am so privileged as to share your bed intimately, then I will share it with the woman I love. No other possibility exists."

The morning found Ada tangled up with Emerly in the sheets, heavy exhaustion still pressing down upon them both.

And with the light, clarity.

Emerly woke her up with gentle kisses, apology as he withdrew his arm from beneath her.

Grinning, he clasped his hands together before sending a finger directly into his chest.

Marry me.

She brought her finger to her lips before bringing an open hand down to meet her fist, an indelible smile on her lips.

I promise.

And she knew just how it'd be done, too.

For who better than a schooner captain to help them swear the holiest of vows?

Chapter 10

EMERLY

Emerly had wanted to spend the morning, dozing beside Ada.

Naked beneath the sheets, her skin warm against his, the anxiety and worry of the Capital beyond had melted into the distance, leaving nothing but hazy satisfaction and heavy eyes behind.

So, naturally, while he was happy for the *reason* they were standing on the dock, watching the ferry dock, Emerly was understandably unenthused to be standing in the cold, woolen cap stifling his mussed hair, gloved fingers laced through Ada's.

The journey across the straight would serve a dual purpose:

First thing was to track down the friend once dear that seemed to have fallen from the face of the earth.

Emerly gave a sigh, breath steaming in the crisp morning air. Whatever sunlight poked through had dissolved, dark clouds enveloping the sky.

Something happened, Ada had insisted earlier that morning. *Emerly, he wouldn't just—just leave, would he?* Her worried eyes had asked a thousand more questions she hadn't dared to voice.

If she let the worries sit in the space between them, they would've been too real, worries like *what if I am not enough* and *what if I cannot be around him anymore, what if this one I once called 'friend' no longer wants to know me?*

It was kind of a sick thing, hunting for permission.

But she was a shrewd judge of character, he told himself, steadying his steps as they stepped onto the ferry. Ada didn't run with traitors.

The second thing was predicated on finding Sebastian, namely because Ada wished to be married by her sweet friend who'd kept her just a bit less lonely those handful of winters she'd spent in the Capital.

"Where are you going," the lips of Ada's mom had frowned, eyes locking on Emerly's and then Ada's, hands gesturing a signal like clock-clogs to inquire about schedules.

"I am to catch a ferry cross the straight and elope with dear Emerly," Ada had shrugged, bringing the words into her hands.

Her mother had simply rolled her eyes, frown relaxing as she picked up to the daily paper once more.

She'd taken it for a joke.

And Ada would *never* let her live that down.

Not when they'd be coming back to the Capital as husband and wife.

Chapter II

SEBASTIAN

A BELL CLANGING ACROSS THE SMALL TOWN PULLED SEBASTIAN FROM the fishing nets he'd been repairing as he sat on the shore, talking with Lee.

It was what they did.

She'd hang lazily off of the rocky outcropping, or else, in the warmer months, float easily with him in the sun.

But nevertheless, it had been an odd way to spend his final hours on land.

He should've been running on the beach.

Climbing the ruins.

No matter.

Soon, he'd sink himself into the saltwater to swim with her.

Soon.

The bell tolled once more, marking mid-morning, and he rose, letting the net slide recklessly into the sea.

"It's time," he breathed, eyes locking on Lee's. "Go."

She said nothing.

She merely gave a curt nod, and dove off, into the water, to swim far beyond the wreckage of the peninsula.

But where her destiny was to fly, and fast, his was to linger.

To stand on the precipice of ending.

To watch the earth split, the symptom of a shattering dream, when this place had been dreamed together, the cracks of eyelids opening to awake, and he would see it.

Magic.

Smoke and Sebastian filled the air as an ear-splitting roar pierced the rock, and from their hidden spot along the shore, he could see it.

The ruins, beginning to fall.

And with it, memories.

The cupola of the Citadel came crashing down, and Sebastian was a child, pretending to be Prae Sebastian, a valiant *vora* warrior.

What of the stained glass?

Only a handful of colored panes had withstood the war, but surely, the first quakes must've knocked the windows out.

He'd marveled at them, as adolescence dawned.

Tried to paint out in his mind's eye, or if time permitted, in the sea glass on the beach, the pictures of the gods that had once graced the Citadel, tried to imagine what it must've been like to see the stretches of red and yellow and green and blue in the morning light—

Sebastian's cheeks were damp with tears as he watched the pieces of the stone wall starting to drop into the sea.

I hope you understand, Lee.

I am giving my soul to the sea.

He'd walked, as a young man, amid the ruins of books, nothing more than sun-bleached pages and rotting leather covers, and he'd wondered whether the brave souls who'd died on this forgotten rock, the ones who'd penned the faded stories, who'd lived through battles, battles legend said were warred by the gods themselves, he wondered if it'd been worth it, to them.

If, in their last moments, they'd regretted what it'd come to, with the war, and all.

He always thought they would have liked what the island became.

That it drifted far from the corruption of the Guild, peaceful and easy.

That in the shadow of destruction, life carried on.

He wanted to take the seas.

Ride them high, and dive to their depths, to chase after the disappointments that the shadows cast down.

He did not want the quiet life.

He did not want peaceful life, easy and mundane.

He loved the days on the schooner with his father and his sister and his mother and he loved the afternoons on the beach mending the fishing nets and he wanted *adventure.*

To yell to the sky, to make the water stand and deliver.

To live.

Another great tremor was send through the earth

Some men, they were destined to tear the ground apart. They would rip the boulders from mountainsides, split the seams of their very world, because some men—some men were dirt.

He'd heard that, once.

Sebastian was not of the soil.

He was of the sea.

He was a man of salt and wind.

And this was the beginning.

Chapter 12

LEE

Through the waves, the whine of splitting stone sent her ears ringing.

He was making a mistake.

She had spent her life alone, condemned beneath the water by her love of life for the humor of the gods, and he was being an absolute *fool*.

And she wasn't his keeper.

Love didn't matter.

Love was a feeling, deep in her gut, that pulled her through to the surface each day to greet the sun, a feeling so strong it made her heart sing and her would-be feet dance and it turned her gods-damned lonely world upside down.

Maybe the gods were laughing with their puppet-hermit, making her swim in the sea she'd loved to death.

But when they'd cursed her to the ocean, they'd done nothing more.

They'd laid out no contract of true love like the tales of her childhood.

There was no bargain to be had, where if she loved enough or kissed the right person or waited for the long years, she was going to live again.

Sebastian had walked the earth for twenty gods-damned years.

If he wanted to walk right into the sea on a wave of rubble because he fancied himself adept at magics that had lived too long in the island's memory, that was his gods-damned prerogative.

Nowhere in the threads of this unraveling was it laid out that she was the one to talk sense into his head.

That was a responsibility laid on others.

But not her. Not her, and not because of her love.

Loving wasn't the same as saving.

He'd watch his beloved Citadel and his beloved memories, his beloved gods-damned *soul,* tumble into the waves.

And when he was still standing on the shore in the company of a madman come morning, he would see.

Banking left for the northern sandbars, Lee dove, furious—

Something was around her.

Seaweed.

That was her first thought, a tangle of oceanfingers reaching up to snare her in her distraction, but a painful *snap* across her cheeks, arms seized—

A rogue fishing net.

Dropped from a schooner.

Where it came from didn't much matter, though.

She was trapped.

Trapped, and the rumble of dirt and rubble and ruin hitting the sea was echoing in the depths.

No, no, no—

It wasn't the first tight spot she'd been in, alone in these waters.

But the more she struggled, the more she fought, screamed lungfuls of water into the sea, panic closed in.

Panic, because she was drifting.

Maybe she'd been swept into the net, but the net was free, happily carried along in the currents below.

And wasn't that the damn irony.

Crying, the ropes starting to dig into her skin and scales the more she struggled, and this life had been a fucking *joke.*

Have your comedy, she screamed, angry into the sea.

The water was growing warm around her, and she could see where the perilous sea floor had split in spite of the plumes of sand and rubble muddying the water, could see that great monstrous cavern afire beneath the waves.

And from the cavern, something inky and dark.

A single, squirly leg, drawing itself through the sand, the prying of a massive creature trying to pull itself to rising, and then another.

In the ocean shadows, a great bulbous creature, rising.

It was beyond even the most terrifying night terror.

Frantic, Lee was tearing at herself, at the net that swept her towards the chasm, screaming to no one—

This is what you brought, Sebastian.

Look what you've done.

You foolish boy.

You would not listen.

And now, I will die.

Chapter 13

ADA

The swell of darkness had come out of nothing.

One moment, Ada had been standing on the ferry barge, pondering Emerly's question about why the gulls had stopped darting through the air, picking and pecking up and down the island coast, the next, the ferry had lurched, someone had screamed, and they were in the water

"Help!" Ada's voice echoed, panicked, into the haze.

It'd been a childish hope, that brought them here.

Sebastian's letters had stopped, the Guild chambers were ringing with futile anger, and gods, it had been *years* she'd spent, wondering how to quantify, clarify, *realize* her feeling for Emerly, years that were answered as the candle light faded into the night and she'd fallen asleep to the sound of his breathing and the feel of his fingers between hers.

It made sense, now.

Wife.

Husband.

The words tangled together in her mind, her cheeks damp with tears as she pulled herself up out of the harbor, coughing.

A great dark wave, stinking of rotten fish and decay, had overtaken the harbor, overtaken the town, and a moment later, the ferry had overturned, lolling helplessly in the water.

It'd been a storming day, no question, but a squall like this, from nowhere—

Someone's hand was around her arm, helping her out.

Emerly.

Thank the gods.

It'd been no small mercy, to be upended in the harbor, fetid though the water may be.

Stranded in the straight in heavy winter clothes, survival would have been unlikely.

Her relief was short-lived, though.

Chaos encircled them. Warning bells clanged across the harbor, the sound of distant screaming—wailing—filling the air. Dogs were barking, men screaming—

"There," someone shouted, pointing, running towards nobody and everybody, all at one. "Over there! There's a man on the shore, he's yelling for help, he says the hermit's lost his mind! He said something about bad magic—"

Magic.

Her heart dropped.

Ada glanced to Emerly, turning the townsman's words over in her hands before gesturing to follow.

His eyes were dubious as he shook his head.

She stole a moment, then.

To meet his gaze.

"We have to go. We have to help. We promised," she signed,

desperate.

Because hadn't they? Her family?

They'd promised Acquisition. Distinction. Protection.

Should any seek to harm our people, our homes, our land, and our souls, they shall answer to me.

Ada had been little, when she'd watched her father swear the vows.

When he'd lifted her onto his leather chair in the guild chamber.

She'd said the words back as best she could.

As his daughter, as a true member of his family, she would be expected to uphold the words, too.

The duty of fealty does not fall on one alone.

She'd asked him to swear her in again, that spring.

When she'd come to his office in their home in the Coastal Reach, and told him her truth.

What is it, my son, he'd asked.

I am no son, she'd said, tears in her eyes. *Dad, I've always been your daughter. I see this, now.*

He'd done nothing. Nothing but, tears in his eyes and a massive smile across his lips, given her a tiny nod. *My apologies. What is it, my daughter?*

Nobody had asked her to swear the vows again.

But she'd wanted to, standing there, in the chambers.

A declaration that she, Ada Follerey, would hold herself, her heart, in solidarity with Aerdela. That, time and again, as she found herself, she would find herself with Aerdela.

And district or no, these people were their kin.

"Please, Emerly."

Will you come with me, she wanted to ask, but there was no time.

Will you love with me and fight with me and heal with me and run with me into the unknown.

Because whatever this was, it wasn't one of the ordinary winter squalls that swept the shores of the island and the Capital alike.

No, a storm wouldn't have plunged this little harbor town into chaos.

And it certainly wouldn't have sent the ground beneath her feet rumbling.

Fear was rising in her chest as she held Emerly's scared gaze.

This should have been her last chance to seize her freedom. To take that boy's hand and run to the island in the name of adolescence that was running short.

Whatever she'd intended this trip to be, she hadn't wanted to face her duty on these shores. She'd wanted an escape. Just one gods-damned day where she could savor irresponsibility.

But magic, she suspected, had a mind of its own.

"Emerly, if it's magic, we have to see," she begged, her fingers clumsy. "I have to know. If I'm ever going to protect Aerdela, I have to know! Please!"

The answer was a small nod.

That moment, she could recall, that felt like a mound of bricks had been lifted from her chest.

"Okay." Emerly gave the small sign of confirmation, brushing his shoulder, symbolic sharing of a burden carried. And they were running.

Chapter 14

EMERLY

There was a man, pointing at the shore, yelling something to Ada, and as he did, she put the words into her hands for Emerly.

The chaos enveloped the shore, but there was something else, something hot and uncomfortable burning deep inside Emerly's chest, something that in another life he'd have called magic, something that anymore could only be called a healing touch, the likes of which he'd inherited from his father.

There was panic all around them, unquestionably, but for what Emerly could see, the squall that had overtaken them had mercifully spared the town proper, and though he hadn't known the sensation of loss often, there was no loss of life or limb amid the squallor.

But beyond the town, towards where the man was beckoning them...

Loss of soul, was the phrase that stuck in Emerly's mind.

It was the sensation of complete and utter loss of self.

The air cut through the damp clothes, and he was running, following both the frantic man and Ada through the muddied street that drizzled out just past the harbor to nothing more than sand and stone. Tall beach grasses whipped in the wind, and as the chaos of the harbor town was left behind them, a picture of ragged destruction blossomed before Emerly's eyes.

Bits of stone and wood poked up in the distance from angry waves, sloughs of mud sliding into the water, or perhaps it was the water encroaching to swallow the land, but bit by bit, the island was being devoured. Ada had talked about it, the way the land curved like a tail, palatial ruins at the tip, but any evidence of such a place was now gone.

And in the path of destruction, two figures.

One, a young man, breath frosting on too-cold air, the other, an elder in ragged robes with hands outstretched.

Emerly glanced back, to where the town lay behind the berms.

This whole island was liable to be eaten up, if the water kept pushing closer, the waves growing ever taller to swallow the next swath.

Ada came to a stop, out of breath, no more than twenty feet from the boy and the elder. Hair soaking, curls gone, she was shivering—though this seemed to be the only evidence of discomfort.

She had been raised to lead a district.

And what are you doing here, boy, a small voice in the back of Emerly's mind demanded.

Standing by the one I love. For isn't that what we do, when the world is ending.

The sea may swallow us whole, but would that we not see the end alone.

Two lines from Ada's favorite book.

A faint smile was tugging on his lips, watching her take a step forward.

She was salt and sun, that girl.

We will not see the end alone.

Chapter 15

SEBASTIAN

"AND SO, WE GIVE TO THE WAVES, AND SO, THEY CONSUME."

The voice of the hermit croaked from behind Sebastian, and he started, turning on his heel.

The old man watched him with beady eyes, rags almost falling off his skin-and-bones frame, fingers poised at the ready. The tips of his ears poked through the gray-almost-white hair, wiry with age and stained with salt, and there was something metallic in the ashen air.

"It's done," Sebastian breathed, taking a step back.

"It is *not,*" the hermit hissed, darting forward. "Someone else has claimed this rite."

His fingers found Sebastian's arms with terrifying strength, pinning him easily to the ground.

Stale breath filled his nose, rotting teeth clacking out the words with spit and venom. "Do you know why I was banished? Do you know, boy? Answer me!"

"No." His voice was a whisper lost in the din.

The hermit heard, though.

"I guard the split! They buried the shadows beneath us all, and I broke my covenant to bury the shadows!"

"I—*what?*"

But the time for reason had passed.

Gone were the moments amid the ruins where the hermit could spill words until the sun sank well below the water.

The air had gone still around them, a deadly ice rising from the earth below.

"Do you know what I do, boy? I rend the flesh! Some mend, I rend, mend, rend, mend, rend..." He left Sebastian pinned to the ground, tethered with invisible threads, a single finger deigning him to stay as the hermit paced. "Mend, rend, mend, rend..."

"I kept my promise!" Sebastian was struggling, now, fighting bonds he could not see. "I gave you the asking price!"

The hermit's head snapped over. "You think your precious memories will buy you fins? You think you were the only one with a claim?"

"I—"

"You think because I rend the flesh you wish to mend, I can shape you into whatever you fancy!" the hermit spat. "Wrong!" He took up pacing again, rolling his shoulders in agitation. "It is old magic! Dark magic! You look into the mirror, and the mirror you become, mirror to the rending, mirror to the rending...should've seen, should've seen..."

Gone.

The old man's mind had gone.

Sebastian was starting to panic, pinned to the ground with the hermit's magic, listening to the sound of ruins and earth beneath sliding into the sea.

He *understood* magic. He knew about blood-pacts and gods and the deep, dark magic of the ocean—

What the *vora* could do, surely it transcended myth, and on this island, where the magic had come to clash, where the aftershocks of conflict had been felt so vastly through the centuries—

"What is done is done," the hermit hissed, "and even I cannot undo a pact written in blood—these fools, they know not what they do—perhaps it is not so foolish—I was the fool, I was the fool..."

Sebastian's thoughts turned to Lee.

Lee, and what he'd promised.

That she wouldn't have to be alone.

That they would take the seas together, and conquer.

Lee, and the memories he'd sank into the ocean for her.

Maybe it was a loss—it had to be, no question—but what greater sacrifice could he make? What greater gift could he give than to consign himself and his obsessions to the waves?

In his heart, a tug.

Beneath his fingers, a deep chill, fending back the fire brought forth by an angry earth.

Lee.

With a scream, Sebastian arched his back, searing pain ripping through his chest as magic he had not known roared to life.

The thought of her.

The thought of their moments on the beach.

How he'd spent his life wandering his lonely fantasies of wars gone by, and she'd swam through the ruins of a life she couldn't have, and maybe they'd both been lost, in their own ways.

His thoughts had turned to why it was he wanted to dive into the water with her, and he was starting to understand the hermit's babbling, now, an icy impetus to move curling in his veins.

You look into the mirror, and the mirror you become.

Lee was right.

Lee had fucking been right.

What the hermit had promised for the sacrifice of the ruins had been impossible.

And the question remained.

What do I see in the mirror.

The stones cracked beneath his hands, and the bonds frozen with magic began to give way.

What do I see.

A man.

Passionate. Full of life. Willing to bring the world down for a little bit of love to go on.

Willing to make Lee's life less lonely.

To make her nights less cold.

The skittering of frost across water crackled through the air, something glacial roaring across the rocky shore.

What do I see.

A frozen determination, the kind he'd seen in his father's eyes.

Chilled looks of reprimand that brought naysayers to heel.

What do I see.

Ice.

Pure. Ice.

Chapter 16

LEE

THE SEA MONSTER STRETCHED, A DEEP ROAR FILLING THE TRENCH, A beast arisen after slumber.

Inky water was bleeding from every crack and crevasse, and still, Lee was trapped.

What fools, the gods were.

Thinking they could play the lives of mortals out like a two-copper drama.

But something happened, then, something Lee could not be sure even the gods could've foreseen, in all their pitiful wisdom.

I loved the sea to death.

She really had, hadn't she.

It was a stunning thing, the sea of her childhood. The way the waves of the Cove would hit the sun just right, blinding all but the most wary and seasoned swimmer. And gods below, it was too cold to be swimming, most of the time, and it didn't matter, because Lee loved the ocean.

From the first time she'd dipped her toes in.

Through the admonishments of her parents.

Past summers wasted away, friends waiting with trepidation on the shore, amid it all.

Lee loved the ocean.

Loved it to death.

And maybe she'd love the creature to death, too.

Maybe the gods would think it funny.

The girl who loved the world straight to dying.

She could love this massive urchin, it's puffing cheeks and spiny whispers, it's squiggled legs that seemed to play the part of fins but barely, tickling the sunken sand dunes as it heaved itself into being.

Loved it because it was a beast, acting upon instinct as it waddled across the sand, stirring up debris, letting out a great screech that set the sediment swirling. Loved it because being here, right here, trapped in this net, being here with fins for feet, being here, beneath the waves—it had been written.

To be caught with a diadem upon her forehead and a locket around her neck, or free in the sea she loved.

It had been Lee, who'd waded into the ocean that day.

She'd known the risks.

She knew, too, that however lonely and cold her fate had been, it had been better to swim along the bay than walk the path she'd been born to.

It had brought adventures instead of meetings with advisory counsels, songs set to the crashing whitecaps for lines hummed to a strumming lyre, a quiet view of the world so grand and mysterious that she could not quite regret the day her head had dipped below the waves.

Magic.

So, Lee went right on, loving that monster.

Loving what grand adventure it seemed to summon from the depths.

And slowly, her net began to fall away.

Piercing eyes unblinking on the urchin, and the net began to loosen, shaken off, off, off with each thunderous rumble of the urchin's feet against the sand.

Run. Go. Swim away, don't look back.

And then what?

The island. Sebastian had foolishly loosed a storm into the depths of the sea, and he *would* be returned to the ocean.

Him, and everyone else on that island, and they wouldn't meet it with fins and scales.

They'd meet it dead.

I love you I love you I love you

She steadied herself against the current, watching as the urchin stumbled, it's thin leg giving way beneath it.

You are everything.

You are the remnants of a split in our world so small only the dreams crept through.

Just like the legends.

You are what the Dreamer dreamt, the nightmare in the dark, the vision of something so vast and terrifying that it could not be contained within a dream any more.

You are the vastness of the stars, the deep trenches of the sea, the impossibility of seeing the world through a tiny peephole and wondering what else lays just beyond the corner of your eye.

You are everything that I love about this life.

A whine set her bones aching, and the urchin came tumbling down into the sand, obscured in a plume of smoke.

You are remarkable.

And I will love you to death.

Chapter 17

ADA

"Sebastian!" Ada's voice echoed, breaking across the beach icy and barren. "Sebastian, answer me!"

A scream of anguish was her only reply.

Sebastian's back was arched, fists clenched as he let out a roar, held seemingly by nothing more than the outstretched hand of the hermit, gray rags fluttering in an unfelt breeze.

What hell had been unleashed here.

No letters, and she'd assumed he was out to sea.

The ground was trembling, terrified beneath her feet, and Ada watched in horror as the earth split, what was left of the ruins of the Citadel tumbling into the sea below.

But it didn't stop there.

Muddy waves were swallowing the shore, edging closer beneath storming skies.

And what am I to do.

Emerly was fond of recalling her talents in the Guild chambers, the way she could traverse even the most perilous verbal traps with ease.

Wit wouldn't carry her far, standing on the brink of destruction.

The sea cared not for humor.

If she could just—just distract the hermit long enough—

"Hey!" Her strides were quick, deliberate as she made for the old man.

The icy winds cut through the soaked apparel, chilling her to the bone—cold, it was too cold, even for this time of year—

The hermit paused, fingers frozen above Sebastian, looking askance at Ada.

Odd.

He was...odd, with his flashing eyes, his ears not quite right—

And in a split-second, he'd turned on her.

His fingers gripped the air, and she was stuck mid-step.

Hoarfrost was crawling beneath her boots, quick breaths frosting the air—

And a moment later, everything was gone.

The world was quiet.

Hazy.

"Take me back." Ada's words were distorted. Distant.

They'd been pulled beneath the surface of a mirrored meadow lake.

"Where am I."

The hermit's eyes locked on her. "In the moments between sleep and waking. In the moments where dreams are born and die with but a heartbeat's notice."

Panic was rising in her chest. "Take me back!"

"You were born with a dream—"

"Take me BACK!" Her scream echoed into nothing, drifting away.

"Listen to me." The hermit's voice snapped her attention back on him. "You were born with a dream. I can see it, in your eyes. Uncontained." He clicked his tongue. "Some of your kind, they turn the world cold. They lift the earth itself. They light the world afire, the mend hearts and hurts, they even tiptoe across the edge of your thoughts, and you—you think you're ordinary. You, though—you've been given such a gift. The gift of the Dreamer. You were born with a dream. Like eyelids cracked open, you see. You see the dreams. You reach through, you reach across the stars, and you pull down from the heavens dreams that make your soul sing, and I—I am your vessel. You touch the stars. You will make them yours." His eyes were glistening, hands keeping them frozen beneath the surface. "It is a long way to reach, though, to pull a star from heaven." A kind smile edged at the corners of his lips. "I serve the dreamers like you. The beautiful people that are radiantly uncontained."

Tears were cold against her cheeks, and she shook her head. "I don't understand, please..."

"You made a pact with the gods," the hermit said softly. "You have not always been called Ada, have you, child? You took your new name and you swore on your life to protect your people in that grand stone hall. And in that hall..." He clicked his tongue. "Did you not shed your own blood with the wish that your people would forget?"

"I..." Ada's mouth fell open in horror.

She had.

She'd sworn the vows in the Guild chambers. And hadn't it been only yesterday, she'd sliced her hand open as she bitterly wished that magic so fierce and deadly had not been the legacy of the continent.

The hermit gave a soft chuckle. "That poor boy had wished to make use of the ruins. The ruins, brimming with scrolls and tomes and memories of magic *you* wished the world to forget."

And Ada didn't quite know how it was possible, but in the space of a teardrop, a world.

It tumbled down off her cheek, and it consumed her.

The lives of those before her.

The others who'd reached the stars.

A flood, and how had she not seen it, before now? How had she not seen that she'd been born with water around her ankles, the tide edging up, up, up with the years—

And she understood.

"I'm...a dreamer." The words were a tear-soaked whisper. "I'm a dreamer, because I haven't always been called Ada."

"My duty is to you. Not that foolish boy sitting on the shore, his head full of fish-wishes. Say the word, and I can help undo the blood-pact you've made." His eyes locked on hers. "Are you sure you wish the memory of magic housed in the Citadel to stay waterlogged on the ocean floor? Books of curses, the accounts of the gods, instructions to wield magic even your dear boy hasn't conceived of—an entire world will be gone."

Aerdela could try to forget.

But sooner or later, someone would find the wreckage of the Citadel. The ruins of the war. And gods only knew what horrors they'd find.

If a drop of blood could bring this storm, who knew what could be done with tangible recollections.

But magic foul and fierce would not be her legacy.

"Let it fall," she breathed.

And the bubble burst.

Chapter 18

EMERLY

HEART POUNDING, EMERLY TRIED TO MOVE.

Tried to scream, tried to run, to reach her—

But where Ada stood before was, for the space of a heartbeat, nothing but a ghost, her and the hermit, like they'd been washed out by the wind leaving nothing but memory.

Like a watercolor painting that been bled of ink.

The fire in his chest flared—

He stopped fighting.

He felt it, deep in his bones, knew it without pause or question.

Wherever she was, she was okay.

He blinked, though, and there she was, and he wondered if it'd simply been the chaos and fear, playing tricks on his mind.

It wasn't.

She turned to him, panting, fingers flying. "How long were we gone?"

Emerly signaled an exhalation of air, a gesture to say she'd been gone for no longer than a breath. "Just a moment."

"He pulled me underneath...something. The world, maybe. Emerly, he's dangerous—"

The fire flared again in Emerly's chest, magic sparking in his palms.

This feeling—this, he knew.

Ada let her hands fall, at a loss as she shook her head, and she must've sensed it, too.

Death.

He'd felt it, when his grandmother died, felt it once, waking up on a cold night not a handful of weeks ago, the first night in the Capital, and he'd risen, brow damp with sweat, out of breath, and what had he done but quietly click open the door of their adjoining rooms, doing his best not to wake her, but to make sure the steady rise and fall of her chest sent the blankets gently stirring.

But it was unmistakable, on these shores, drifting up from the half-freezing waves.

A fifth would keep them company, the fire in his chest whispered.

Death would join them soon.

Chapter 19

SEBASTIAN

Cold was seeping across the ocean waves, freezing the tempestuous whitecaps into twisted glass.

And Sebastian was free from whatever bonds the hermit had used to pin him to the shore.

He'd felt the hold starting to give, somehow, cold twists of imagined iron unraveling, until finally, they'd snapped.

But it was not the breaking by force, he reflected warily, rolling onto his side, catching his steaming breath, bracing himself to rise.

He had been set free.

What am I.

Ice.

He was ice.

Sebastian watched a fractal pattern crawling out beneath where his fingers clawed into the half-frozen sand.

The ground gave another tremor beneath him.

He had done his part, Sebastian thought furiously, pushing himself back to unsteady feet. He'd given his memories to the sea, and for what?

For the ice?

The toe of his boot met the sand in fury, sprays of frozen chunks flying through the air as a cry of frustration left his lips.

Sebastian turned, ready for the clash, ready to make that gods-damned fool pay—

No

It was a split-second.

A blink of the eye, hardly a breath, but—

It was her.

Ada.

Ada, in her plaid calico skirt, hem half-frozen, her high-collared jacket, her dark brown hair grown already down to her jaw, sodden, cheeks flushed with the cold—

Ada, and she'd come to the island. He hadn't written back, and she'd come looking for her friend.

Her eyes were locked on the hermit, vacant.

"No!"

A shuddering chill split through his chest, spilling into the world.

Not Ada. He wouldn't let the hermit take her, wouldn't let her fall simply because she simply couldn't leave well enough alone—

Maybe it was his voice that snapped her from his grip.

Somehow, though, he didn't think so.

Powerless.

The notion hit him squarely in the chest.

Maybe that was the joke, all along.

Maybe that was actually what he saw he looked in the mirror.

A man who'd spent his life at the mercy of his own imagination. Who pushed everyone else out of his life until he'd had no recourse but to seek refuge in the fairy tales. The hermit could only rend one into their reflection, and it must've been easy, then, to bring the earth crashing down into the sea, to summon the power of the sacrifice of memories, to make Sebastian into a man so powerless as he watched everything—everyone—he loved vanish.

He'd been a boy, playing at power.

And anymore, he was a man, stripped of any such imaginings.

Moving, he felt the ground begin to crack and crumble beneath his shoes, his own icy temper at last unleashed.

"Sebastian, *no!*" Ada's voice cut through the storm.

She'd moved between Sebastian and the hermit, blocking his fury.

Foolish girl.

"Move," Sebastian snarled, taking a step forward. "Ada, you don't understand—"

"I don't know what you're trying to do here, Sebastian." She looked warily to the other man on the beach, the one Sebastian didn't know, her fingers spelling words as she spoke. "I don't know why you wouldn't write me back, I don't—" She swallowed, shaking her head. "But you are going to tell me. *Right. Now.*"

Chapter 20

LEE

LEE PRESSED A FIST TO HER MOUTH, WATCHING IN HORROR AND relief as the urchin tumbled back into the chasm.

Goodbye.

What a horrific talent, to love a thing to death. It didn't matter if it was hers or the monstrous sea creature.

It was a wretched thing.

Not half so wretched, though, as what took the urchin's place.

A plume of something dark soured the muddy waters, moving with unnatural pace, some vile ink flying up, up, up towards the sky far above—

Lee turned tail, swimming violently against the agitated waters.

Whatever she'd traded for the life of the massive shadow urchin, she did not care to see.

There were some things that didn't warrant her love.

It was a powerful thing, that much was clear.

And it was hers.

Sebastian.

A surge of panic sent her through the water, an arrow aiming for the surface.

Sebastian, and his wretched plan—

He was going to be inconsolable. Crashing the earth above, losing the ground he loved so much—and forget whatever hell his sacrifice had pulled from below, forget whatever beast had gorged on the memories of childhood only to be loved to death by a woman beneath the waters.

He would take this as the ultimate failing.

That in spite of it all, they'd spend their lives split by a coast. He would walk along the rocky shores, and she would dive beneath the waves, and he would never learn to be happy with the cards they'd been dealt.

And maybe, that meant his love was just as deadly as hers.

Lee's eyes were focused on the hazy light shining down from the surface—so close, she was nearly there—

But something was wrong.

Where the waves should've been cresting into angry rolls, white foam spilling up, nothing but water sloshing against a thick frozen sheen waited.

Her fists met the ice, furious.

Tendrils of black raced towards the sky, darkening the water behind her, around her—

Her hands were bleeding red into the freezing water as she tried to break through, screaming unheard pleas for *one gods-damned fracture* beneath the glacial sky.

She was shaking, the water growing putrid and stale, each gulping breath down harder and harder to take—

And all she could think was that Sebastian was a fool.

He'd been happy to give the ruins to the sea without sparing a thought for the wretched things that spiraled up, things that feasted upon time itself, that devoured down happy memories of yester-year.

He didn't think that maybe a life divided by sand and sea was better than nothing at all.

Perhaps it was a mercy, she thought bitterly, not ceasing the fight. A mercy that whatever this wretched thing was, it was trapped beneath the ice, for what havoc it would wreak in a world steeped with nostalgia for days gone by.

Above, they still whispered about the magic.

Grandparents, around their fires, whispering about all the wonderful and terrible things that were drawn forth from recollections of their own grandparents around a fire just like that one, and what a feast that might be.

At some point amid the panic and fear, she must've realized.

Sebastian would mourn more than a failed piece of ancient magic.

He was trying to wrap his fingers around a world he didn't understand, and it was going to end them both.

She loved Sebastian, and she wondered if her love would kill him, too.

If she would love Sebastian to death.

Like the sea, and the monster, and her whole life before.

When the world went dark, Lee knew she was still screaming.

Still fighting.

But as she choked down a final gulp of fetid water, she knew it was over.

All this love had been the death of her.

Chapter 21

ADA

"Tell me what you've done," Ada snarled, finding Sebastian's dark eyes. She was before the hermit, as if it'd be enough to protect the one who could build ladders to those starry dreams above. "Tell me, Sebastian. *Now.*" Ada signed the words, sparing a glance over to Emerly, who gave a nod of understanding.

Sebastian's skin seemed to shimmer in the cold, eyes glistening with grief. "I found a love," he whispered. "And a way out."

Ada pressed her eyes shut, grimacing, pausing a moment to find the gestures to pass the words to Emerly.

Of course.

Of course, Sebastian would be looking for a way off this gods-damned island.

Sebastian had been mourning his own life, when she'd met him on the docks of the Capital, peddling seafood to anyone with enough gold in their pockets to indulge.

It'd taken her time to see it, of course.

Because Sebastian had a laundry list of reasons to be happy, here.

It may have been the Abandoned Island, but it was teeming with life.

Before, it had been what the Merchants wished the Capital to be.

A bustling metropolis, a trading port harboring any and all, and even in its quiet decline, it was a wealth of the remarkable. The enclave of scholars, set away transcribing the old books that were now left sinking to the ocean floor, the natural springs where one might sit and bathe in the mineral water and watch the ships sail by, it seemed, to Ada a dream.

But she never saw it through his eyes.

And to him, it stayed a prison.

That was the trouble, with the dreams of others—they weren't for the eyes of anyone but the dreamer. And when they left the land of sleep to meet the gaze of those already awake, they seemed, to Ada's thinking, to always be nothing but nonsense.

"What way out," Ada breathed, eyes skirting the frozen shores, fingers moving in hesitation. "What way out did you find?"

Whatever he had tried to do, her inadvertent gift of blood to the stone floor of the Guild chambers had interfered.

Sebastian shook his head, thrusting a finger towards the hermit. "He promised. He *promised* he could do this, fix this—and—"

"I cannot see all, boy!" the hermit shrieked, dancing from behind the refuge of Ada's outstretched arms. "Your words were poetic, meaning veiled from even the gods, I cannot stop the dreamer's wish—"

Ada glanced back to Emerly, delivering the hermit's words, watching as he wrapped his arms around his chest in worry.

"Must, must, must go back! The world is forgetting, as it must!" the hermit said gleefully, drumming his fingers together. "They ask for their memories, and their memories, they must have!"

Ada's schoolgirl sign was slow as she tried to piece the hermit's rant together, glancing back at Emerly.

But he was waving her off, eyes widening on the scene unfurling behind her as he bolted forward.

Sebastian was on his knees, coughing in the sand.

"See, see," the hermit chirped, "see—"

"Shut up," Ada muttered, shaking him off as he clawed at her arms with glee. "Sebastian? Sebastian!"

But he was struggling for breath, hand on his chest, pain deep in his eyes.

Collapsing into the sand, his lips shaped words unheard, eyes searching the sky with panic.

Emerly's knees hit the frozen ground beside them both. Ada let her hand rest on Sebastian's shoulder, some attempt at comfort amid the terror—hers, as much as his.

He was dying. Laying there on the frozen shore, dying.

She whirled, fingertips not daring to leave her friend. "What did you do to him?" she snarled, scowling at the hermit, her words breaking through the storm.

"Me?" The hermit prodded a single finger into his own chest, eyes wide. "Me? Nothing—"

"Lies!" Ada's breath was tight in her chest, cold closing in around her.

Soaked to the bone.

Stranded, on this gods-forsaken island amid the hell this hermit had drawn forth.

Crashing ruins and shadows to swallow the memories...

"What did you *do?*" Ada hissed.

"Wouldn't the ocean love to get a nibble of him, him and his memories," the hermit sang, delighted. "Too bad, love, dearling, that he's loved the ocean to death."

Chapter 22

EMERLY

No heartbeat—

Maybe he should've been panicking.

After all, Emerly had watched a man die in front of him, had, even as he'd fumbled to check for breath, for a pulse, felt the life disappear.

No.

No, it simply wasn't a choice.

Ada was signing something of sending memories into the sea, of magic old and grand, and really, all of that was just horseshit.

All that mattered, right now, was the man prone on the sand.

All that mattered, Emerly could remember his father saying, was that there was pain in the world, and those with a duty to negate it.

Lacing his fingers together, he squared the placement above the breastbone, and dropped his weight behind it.

One, two, three, four, five—

They had their own patter to sharing thoughts, he and Ada, a patter that surely included a repertoire of small sounds, the sigh of exhaustion he knew he made, easy laughter that felt so free, murmurs of *love* that had kept them company in the dark of night when the candle had at last burned out. "I will save him." Emerly spared a glance up, vocalizing the words.

"Promise," Ada asked, circling her heart.

He nodded. *Promise.*

Chapter 23

SEBASTIAN

On a distant shore, someone was waiting.

Sebastian knew Ada's hand was on his shoulder, that the boy at her side was laying hot hands on Sebastian's chest, sending hot jolts cracking into ribs, and yet, on a distant shore, someone was waiting.

He'd known how this was supposed to go.

The hermit had lived on the island for ages past, since long before Sebastian had been there, and it'd been Lee, who told Sebastian about the man who'd sent his magic swirling on the banks of the Abandoned Island.

The man that made the gods laugh.

But it wasn't him.

Not really.

Whatever had feasted on the memories feasted on Lee, melding her with the ocean she loved so deeply.

No matter.

The hermit knew the secrets of the shadows.

And now, Sebastian did, too.

He cursed himself, now, watching the distant shore, that it'd taken him so long.

Whatever magic lurked beneath the ocean, lying in wait—it demanded a sacrifice.

It demanded love, affection, memory...

And above all else, a soul.

For what magic might be possible, when the shadows were fed by the souls, living, damned, it made no difference, Sebastian realized, watching the figure on the shore.

He'd been on the island.

He'd left Ada caught between the hermit and himself, and then his knees had hit the sand.

The figure in the distance crossed her arms, frowning as she watched.

Not beckoning him.

But she didn't shoo him away, either.

Sebastian could've stayed adrift there, he felt. Caught in between for the rest of time.

It was peaceful, in a way.

The fussing on one side.

The quiet still of the beyond on the other.

Time, to simply wonder what had gone so tragically wrong.

Lee would be waiting, back home.

Would it ever be enough.

Those few hours his fingers slid through hers, the soft touch of her lips against his cheek, the easy way she'd grin, squeezing his hand before letting go, how, how could it sustain a lifetime.

He felt a jolt through his ribs, and reflexively, put a hand to his chest.

With ease.

It could sustain a lifetime with ease, if that was all she could give.

Sebastian swallowed, eyes starting to sting his cheeks.

Hot.

It was so hot, here—no.

No, that couldn't be right—

The in between seemed to be waning.

No. No, I'm not ready to leave, not ready to—to stay—

Then, there was Ada.

Ada, and she had simply blossomed, from those years back on the docks, when they'd sit and shoot the breeze and talk about the Capital and the Merchants and how brilliantly dreadful it all sort of was, even though it wasn't, really. Fingers chilled, noses red, cheeks flushed with winter and it had been lovely.

Really, truly lovely.

Just like her.

In another life, he supposed.

She'd always loved Emerly. And Emerly, from the sound of it, had always loved her.

Sebastian couldn't stay on the island.

The thought seemed to rip away the freezing pain of the banks, luring him back.

It didn't matter how much he loved the rest, or how each of them in turn offered enough love to keep him going.

That place had been hell, and without the refuge of the ruins...

Well.

Part of him had died, when they'd crashed into the ocean.

And maybe it'd been okay, thinking that the wreckage of his childhood would feed something fantastic. Thinking that it'd fuel something better, something beyond those desolate moments where he'd walk through the annals of history, begging to live anywhere but the now.

But sometimes, ruins were just ruins.

A relic of something he'd never see.

Chapter 24

LEE

"WAKE UP."

Lee was aware, at least to a degree, of a shore.

But more than that, of air, biting against damp skin.

Of voices.

And in the distance, laughter.

She opened her eyes, and it was Death before her, once more.

"This has been fun," Death said, a smile dancing on her lips. "But I think we're about done, here." She opened a small box, and something hot filled Lee's lungs, setting her whole body afire.

Her soul, returned from Death.

Death's smile softened, as Lee writhed in pain. "Would that we all had someone to hold our soul safe while we make navigate the currents," Death said quietly. Then, with a sweep across Lee's stinging eyes, the world was dark.

Chapter 25

ADA

Still shivering, Ada sighed, reluctant to shed the blanket around her.

The roughspun wool had been tossed across her shoulders at some point, when or by who, she did not know.

It had to have been after, bleary-eyed, Emerly had looked up from where Sebastian lay prone on the sand, tears on his cheeks.

Then, too, it had to have been after the hermit had screamed, seeing the body of a woman washed up upon the shore. He'd run screaming towards the ice-capped waves, yelling even as the ice had cracked and he'd been plunged beneath the freezing sea.

And it must've been after Ada had fallen back on her heels, trying to catch breaths that would not come.

After she'd, even then, instructed the bystanders to take Sebastian's limp body back to the harbor town, hidden beyond the docks themselves behind the ancient seawall.

So, surely, it had been when they'd surveyed the desolation of the island.

It hadn't been as bad as she'd thought, Ada had reflected. The ruins had been abandoned by scholars and sailors alike, but even so, such a fracture should've shaken the island.

The waves, the chaos, the ice—it should've overtaken the town.

A red-headed woman had kissed a silvery token on a necklace, murmuring some gratitude, though, and it was clear, whatever god these people prayed to had come through.

It was funny, in a way.

Before, that phrase—*whatever god these people prayed to had come through*—it would've been the sort of meaningless thing any skeptic said.

It was impossible to deny that something otherwordly lurked here.

Had, too, been dwelling in the Capital.

In the hands of her lover.

The lodgings were unlike anything she'd seen.

Hot spring water, piped into a great stone tub easily large enough for two, was the feature of the bathing room, indeed, the entire room itself. Mosaic tiles depicted a sandy shore, black-tiled waves curling up where the water in the tub peaked towards the lip, and Ada was lost in the pattern.

What happened.

Emerly's hand on her shoulder brought her back.

His eyes met hers before flicking to the tub, now filled with steaming water, the stench of minerals filling the room.

He'd abandoned his soaking wet tunic, the hair on his chest damp and matted to his clammy skin, his pants sitting low on his hips, buttons already undone.

"Are you okay?" Emerly's fingers moved stiffly, the cold lingering in his bones.

She shrugged, letting him take the wool blanket.

No.

Yes.

Who knew.

Emerly made a gesture as if he were unbuttoning his own shirt, and he raised an eyebrow, lifting his palm up to support something unseen. "Do you need help?"

She gave a small nod.

Her thoughts turned to the hermit, and she let Emerly slide one arm, then another, from the blouse before abandoning it to the floor.

"This was my fault," Ada signed, pulling away from Emerly to catch his gaze for just a moment. One glance down her chest, down her body, and then she looked back to Emerly, who clearly understood the meaning.

"No."

She shrugged, loosening the belt that held the sodden skirt in place. Then—

"When I cut my hand on my belt, yesterday, watching Father in the chambers, ranting about magic and shadows." Her fingers were stiff with cold as she moved the words to being. "The hermit said I invoked a blood-pact. I wished for everyone to forget magic."

Emerly frowned. "Maybe. But the fact remains. He and Sebastian were up to something."

Ada sighed, moving for the tub.

The future was terrifying.

Blood-pacts could be made with the slip of a hand. Land could slide beneath the waves, good people could die, cold and alone and heartbroken, and she could not see a way forward.

Ada had witnessed the dangers.

Seen the loss.

And she would be her father, ranting on the Guild chamber floor about how dangerous it was to set loose a power her people did not understand.

The hot water made her melt, prickling almost uncomfortably against her skin as she slid into the tub. Hair pulled into a messy bun, stray strands curling in the heat, she reveled in the relief.

Emerly slid in beside her, resting his head on her shoulder.

I thought we'd be married, by now, she thought wistfully.

Then, too, they'd scoff at that.

That she'd want to marry some boy from the orchards of the Coastal Reach. Want those sweet memories of her own.

Sebastian had sent his own bittersweet dreams of what could be into the ocean below.

She'd build hers in a townhouse in the winters of the Capital with Emerly.

Her hand found his beneath the water, lacing their fingers together.

Tomorrow, love, she thought, letting the hot water drown her worry.

Chapter 26

EMERLY

EMERLY LET THE HOT BATH ENVELOP HIM.

Tilting his head back against the lip of the tub, he loosed his fingers from Ada's, instead moving to draw her into his arms, body pressed up close against his.

And something snapped.

Whatever had held it all back seemed to vanish, hot tears making his eyes prickle.

Ada's chest heaved, too, her shoulders shaking beneath his arm, and that was how the night left them.

Crying, and praying that the warm water would wash the fear away.

It wasn't wondrous, what had happened on the shore.

There was no delight of satisfaction in realizing that in a moment of heartache, a young boy had asked the hermit to crash half the island down into the sea, misunderstanding the bargain. There was no cause to celebrate, that such old and dangerous magics existed, lingering off the coast of a burgeoning human expanse, brimming with those who had themselves condemned such powers.

Powers, Emerly realized, that lived just as much inside his heart as they did anywhere.

He knew what he'd managed on the beach was no accident.

Perhaps the Guild was fumbling in the departure of the Commissioner who'd staked his fortunes on the luck of the north, but the stories of their grandparents always seemed to disclaim allegations of hardship.

Most folks found a way to get by, as the Guild had emerged from the ruins of the wars.

The heavy truth broke his heart.

Theirs was a world of fragile stability, stability that would come shattering down should the whispers of magic start flying in the streets. Fear had gripped them once before, fear, and the memory of the destruction wrought at the hands of magic, and their world had found a tentative healing.

Negate pain.

Emerly buried his face into Ada's salt-soaked hair, chest tight, face streaked with tears.

They'd be negating pain, alright. Just not his pain.

Chapter 27

SEBASTIAN

He was only aware of pounding.

Someone, in the far away, beating mercilessly on a massive drum.

Not...not a drum.

Blinking, lashes sticky with salt, Sebastian gave a groan, temples throbbing.

He could recall, vaguely, staring at a distant shore.

Now, as he lay cradled into a soft bed, body aching horribly, he wondered what had happened to that woman on the distant shore.

Lee.

He pushed himself to sitting, regretting it immediately as the room started to spin.

It was quiet, despite the roaring in his ears.

Sunlight was just starting to tip through the window, spilling onto the floor, the hint of a chilled dawn rising over the wreckage of whatever remained of the Abandoned Island.

The lodge was vaguely familiar, with the plaster walls, the rope-held shafts drifting down beneath the clay-shingled roof, a cast iron beast of a stove with a glass door chugging plumes of smoke up and out the chimney.

He'd been here, once or twice, just to run the scant errand to the landlady who kept the place.

Of course, they'd have brought him here.

His family would be too far up the shore to drag his unconscious form along a frozen beach amidst the raging storm.

In the haze of coming to, he tried to take inventory of himself.

Of the wreckage.

Lee.

It'd all started with Lee, of course, and the overwhelming urge to flee.

The hermit had promised him fins for legs, or so Sebastian had thought, all for the price of memory and ruin.

Sink the holy relics of a bygone era into the sea, and Sebastian would get a new start.

Sebastian had been naive.

Sinking down into the pillows, he groaned, fingers clawing into his head in discomfort.

He'd simply been a passerby.

And this—this storm, it'd been a waystation in something larger.

He had to find Lee.

They'd figure it out. Somehow. He—he'd build a home on the shore. Carve out a stone pool, deep and wide, talk to his uncle, who'd helped fix the pipes of steaming spring water running through this very lodge when they'd burst a few years back, heat the...the pool...

It felt desperate.

And kind of unfair.

But didn't they have a right to build their home any way they pleased?

Maybe Lee would never be able to leave the waves for long, but he could easily sink into the water beside her, at least for a time. There was no law that said they couldn't drift together in a pool before a fire, or—or share an entire home, split half on land, half against water.

There was no reason that space couldn't belong to them both.

What was a home, anyway, but a safe harbor for souls within.

Finding Lee seemed worlds away, though, at the moment, body aching, room still spinning.

It must've been a light tap on the doorframe, but the knuckles against wood splintered across the room, and Sebastian squeezed his eyes closed, decimated again.

"Heard you stir. How do you feel?" a soft voice asked. The sound of feet padding across the wooden floor, and the brush of clothing as someone shifted, filled the air.

Sebastian forced his eyes open again.

But any breath he'd had in his waterlogged lungs had been stolen away.

He almost didn't recognize her, standing there.

Her blonde hair had been pulled into a herringbone braid, a baggy red sweater and cross-hatched patterned fishermen's long johns replacing what been before.

What had, beneath the waves, been simply scales, and her bare skin.

Lee was grinning, watching him with sparkling eyes. She paused, for just a moment, and then, chuckling, made her way to the bed, crawling in beside him beneath the comforter. "I...owe you an apology," she sighed, propping herself against the headboard.

"Lee, no—"

"I love a lot of things, apparently. Including you." Her smile faltered. "I loved you to death, Lee. That boy—Emerly—he's the one that saved you. Hence, the broken ribs. Well," Lee amended, settling in further, "formerly broken. He said they'd be a little sore. But he's mended you decently, it seems. As best as one can mend someone who's been loved to death. It's...not a terribly good way to love. For either of us."

His hand found hers.

It felt unreal, laying here beside her.

Like any moment, the illusion would be shattered, and he'd awake.

The sensation, though, was replaced a moment later by overwhelming, undeniable guilt.

She'd been ripped from the ocean she loved.

And he wished it to be no different.

"Why are you here," he asked hoarsely, looking at her askance.

She gave a wistful smile. "I...am not of the ocean. And I'm not of the shadows, either. There's something, Sebastian, something deep below. How many of us have mistaken love for promise? Or affection for nostalgia? Even the greatest magics, it seems, are not immune to this fatally human mistake."

"I don't understand." With her help, he sat up, fully meeting her gaze, now.

She only pursed her lips, shaking her head. "The best I can reason? It mistook my love for duty. I loved the sea, Sebastian. But whatever magic is down there thought that just because I loved the sea meant I owed it my life. My *soul.* I guess that's what love means when you're nothing but salt and waves. All-enveloping, all-consuming, until the only thing left is— is nothing," she sniffed, brushing her damp eyes. "And I can't. We need to find a different way to love each other, Sebastian. Okay?"

"Yeah."

She was right.

They needed to love different.

But her words were growing foggy. He let her voice wash over him, fading in and out of focus in an easy ebb and flow.

They sat, quiet, almost nonsense words drifting between them every now and then, the landlady's son stopping in after a time with a plate of food, and queries about how they were fairing.

A strong mug of the landlady's brew, hot and thick, and the world began to fade again.

When sleep finally took Sebastian, it was deep and dreamless.

Peaceful, at last.

Chapter 28

LEE

Anxiety was pressing in, watching Sebastian doze.

Duty compelled her back north, back to her home.

It wasn't really the sea that she'd loved, Lee realized, sitting there beside Sebastian. It was the possibility.

The freedom.

She loved the idea that rules had been broken, that she'd been free from obligation by circumstance instead of by conflict, and now that it had all been righted—supposedly righted—the unsettled feeling of duty returned.

Leaving Sebastian passed out beneath heaps of blankets, snoring softly, she went to wander the lodging.

Ada was in the common room, sipping on a mulled cider, papers spread out before her.

"Keeping busy, I see," Lee sighed, sinking down beside her. "As if you didn't have enough to do?"

Ada gave a mischievous half-smile. "It's calming, working through things. Things at home are simply falling apart, I—I have an amendment to submit for consideration, to the Doctrine, and Father's a disaster..."

Lee pursed her lips. "It's true, then? The expansion?"

"It's true." Ada moved a sheet of paper aside, glancing to Lee. "What's the City going to do, you think?"

"Dunno." Lee gave a half-hearted shrug. "I've been gone for too long to say. Likely nothing." Her eyes locked on Ada's. "How do you know? About the City? I thought you were from the Coastal Reach, only the Merchants..." She trailed off, the rest unnecessary.

Only the Merchants serving in the Guild were rumored to know.

"Father...he's tired. And I am his successor. I believe he is planning on withdrawing his seat, soon. And when he does, I must be ready." She paused. "Is...it likely," she went on, after a moment, choosing her words cautiously, "that you and I shall be friends, beyond this?"

Lee considered the question. "We should certainly be friends," she said at last, "but I do not think we'll have occasion to be professional associates."

Meaning that Lee wouldn't be going home.

She'd more or less known it in her heart, from the moment she'd awoken.

Saying the words, though...

It set her at ease.

A spoken agreement.

She would not be going back.

She would never claim her birthright to the City, hidden in the cove of the northeastern shore, an enclave of magic away from the Guild.

A refuge, from the war now long-since gone.

"Where's Emerly?" Lee asked, not eager to pursue the subject of the City further.

Ada gave a soft chuckle, taking a sip of cider. "Asleep. Healing Sebastian...it took a lot out of him. I expect he'll be out for the rest of the day, at least."

Perhaps a simple statement of fact.

Then, too, though, it was a betrayal of how much, exactly, Ada knew.

She wasn't fumbling for words for what her lover could do.

She knew about the magic.

Of course, perhaps it was a moot point, after today.

Lee blew out a breath. "And you're working."

Ada raised a manicured eyebrow, resting her head in her hand, but said nothing. Her brown curls were loose, pulled half-back. She'd donned a pair of soft stripped long johns, as well, a bulky knit cardigan tossed over a blouse.

"I like the outfit," Lee grinned, leaning against the table. "Especially the stripes."

Ada huffed a laugh. "Yeah. Well. To be honest, I'm not keen to be back in trousers, but there it is."

"Oh?"

Ada clicked her tongue, eyes flitting about the room.

"I'm sorry if I offended you," Lee put forth, frowning.

"No, you...didn't," Ada said, seeming to chose her words carefully. Then, glancing back, she met Lee's gaze. "I...am a different kind of woman. I wasn't born like you. They made a mistake. They thought I was a boy. And it's a kind of convincing lie, sometimes. I didn't realize they'd been mistaken until pretty recently." Her cheeks were flushed, voice soft. "So. Anyway. I've been enjoying not wearing trousers."

There'd been words of reassurance poised on Lee's tongue.

Boys can wear those skirts, too.

You don't have to be a girl to enjoy not wearing trousers.

And for all their would-be truth, they missed the mark. Missed the point entirely, really.

Ada's words were quiet celebration. She'd waded through years of *shoulds* and *should-nots* and found something that made her soul sing, and it didn't do, for Lee to turn around and pick the words to death, for to do so was to say *I do not treasure this victory you've found.*

Lee's mother had done that, one too many times.

Twisted her words away until there'd been nothing beyond suffocating obligation and duty.

What's the point of duty when you're dead, she could remember thinking.

No matter.

She'd loved the sea to death.

Eyeing Ada, there was a grin tugging at the corners of Lee's mouth. "Can I braid your hair?"

Ada nodded, eyes sparkling as she turned her back towards Lee.

"So, what's next," Lee prompted in a low voice, practiced fingers working the strands. She used to braid her sister's hair, once.

But there was death in Lee's family, that much, was undeniable.

And Lee wanted a chance to live.

"What's next," Ada echoed thoughtfully. "Rest, I think. Time to understand. And then, we must figure out what it is we're going to do." She glanced back at Lee. "Magic is swelling up from the sea. That cannot be ignored."

Chapter 29

ADA

Exhaustion had claimed them all, in the end.

Ada had sat with Lee, talking in the main hall, until she'd felt herself losing grip on the world around, until, after mugs of cider and the heat of the roaring fire, she wanted nothing more than to forget this wretched day and abandon them all to sleep.

And yet, the voices seemed a roar in the silent night.

Questions, demands, accusations—from those either too cowardly, or perhaps too ashamed, to admit they did not have the answers, and mistook the young for easy prey.

The din of the Guild Chambers seemed to carry across the straight, across time itself, even, loud in her ears.

Emerly's arms around her did little to settle her worry.

But it was nice, not to be alone with only her anxieties.

Nice, to find a bit of comfort.

They'd come here to be married by an honest-to-goodness sea captain.

It'd been a childish thing, perhaps, to sneak away full well knowing her mother had taken her quip for a joke, to skirt responsibility in the name of a whim Ada knew the others would never understand.

It wasn't *just* the words husband and wife, though those were lovely. And it wasn't just the promise or the pact or the love, or any of the other things that would've been there anyway.

It was a dream.

To stand, in a white gown, holding the hands of the man she loved, an unquestionable display, an announcement to the world that they were *in love,* that he had her back, and she had his, that one could not be double-crossed lest the other seek vengeance, it was to scream to the world *I have another person fighting in my corner,* and everyone always thought that marriage was a vow to the one you were pledged to, that it was the commitment of those to each other, but that was so *wrong,* so painfully wrong, it wasn't that at all, it was a pact made between you and the rest of the world, a pact that said *If you hurt them, if you lie to them, if you get in their way, I will come for you,* a vow sworn to every other living soul that they'd best think twice before hurting the one you loved.

It was, above all else, a warning.

This one is not alone.

For that was how they won, wasn't it? All of the villains in the stories her mother had told her, all the people who'd ever hurt her, wasn't that how they did it?

Corner them, corral them, cut off every lifeline, every love, every person who might've given solace amid the hopeless onslaught.

This one is not alone, though.

I am not alone.

It was with these thoughts that she shifted, sliding Emerly's arm up and around her, resting her head on his chest as he slept.

Chapter 30

EMERLY

THE MORNING FOUND EMERLY ACHING AND SORE AND COVERED IN early sun as light poured unhindered through the curtains of their lodge room.

With a groan, he stretched, legs brushing Ada's along the way as he rolled over, tangling himself with her once more.

The moment of peace was short-lived, as all tiny moments on the morning of a wedding tend to be.

Ada had wanted to walk the coast before they left, to survey the damage.

But beyond evidence of a winter storm, and the missing strip of land that must've surely been there the day before but was now nothing but ocean, there remained no evidence that something had unfolded.

Ada said the hermit called her a dreamer.

Now, watching the island shrink from the deck of the schooner, Emerly was half-inclined to believe that himself.

If this bitter reality had any truth to it, it was that what happened on the island would never serve as fodder for the stories.

Ada tapped his shoulder, her smile bright, light-colored dress fluttering faintly in the breeze despite the heavy, wintered material. Her hair was done up with ribbons and braids—appropriate, for a bride, Lee had grinned.

A thousand things, he might've said to her, in that moment.

Instead, he tucked a stray strand of hair back behind her ear, and letting his hand slide down behind her neck, he leaned in and kissed her.

Wife.

Chapter 31

SEBASTIAN

The morning was crisp and clear, no hint of the storm in the calm waters.

Of course, that the southern tip of the island was missing—this was harder to ignore.

Sebastian sighed, arm around Lee.

The island would remember.

Ada's pale gown snapped in the winds, that girl herself a sail carrying them onward, Emerly at her side.

He'd married them, Ada and Emerly, on the docs of the schooner that morning.

It wasn't trouble, offering to ferry them back across the strait.

It was, in truth, too little time to spend with his friends, in the wake of it all.

But if the island remembered, the sea was impatient, and it would not wait for long.

There was a world brimming with mystery.

He needed answers.

What had happened on the beach had changed him.

He'd been hoping for fins and scales, but what he'd gotten instead touched even the quietest corners of his heart.

Pirate.

Anymore, it was a curse.

But long ago, in the language of their fore-bearers, it'd meant something else.

Peira.

An attempt.

He would try this, this living-with-the-still-alive thing, just for a bit.

Chapter 32

LEE

She had thought about hastily penning a letter, to be curried to the City through Ada's connections.

It made no matter, though.

They'd marked her as dead, years ago.

Ironic, she thought, watching the coastline disappear in the distance.

There'd be others to take her place.

Duty, she'd come to see, was a myth, told by those too afraid to reshape their world beyond expectation.

And so they would sail away, quiet and forgotten, in the name of adventure they'd both been born to chase.

Whether the waves would give them answers, none could say, but at least the water would carry them on, and on, and on, and surely, Lee mused, leaning on the bow of the schooner, surely that wasn't such a bad thing.

To at last be set free.

EPILOGUE

ADA

THE LETTER SAT NEATLY ON THE DESK, BESIDE AN ENVELOPE THAT had been carefully split by gentle hands.

Ada sighed, lifting it again before rising to pace before the tall windows of her upstairs bedroom in the rented Capital house.

Emerly's steps drew her attention, and she tossed the letter aside once more.

"What," he signed, the word hanging in the air between them.

"I got a letter. From Lilah Foster."

"The girl whose father went north," Emerly clarified.

Ada nodded, gesturing Emerly toward the letter. "Take a look."

There is a problem.

No salutation.

No banalities.

There is a problem, Lilah began, *and I fear it goes far beyond this hell of a Basin our Father has trapped us in.*

These hills are crawling with something we cannot understand.

I had a dream, Ada.

A horrible, terrible dream, and I pen these words, praying we will not forget.

And there was nothing left to do, now.

She was caught in a balancing act that would either undo them all, or save Aerdela.

Magic was supposed to be a myth.

Her father, the Guild—they did not understand magic. That it was hardly a thing to be ignored, a fickle child throwing a tantrum after being set away without supper.

They talked of protecting Aerdela.

It was not Aerdela that needed protecting.

These humans, living in a world where magic was myth, they were hardly blameless in the catastrophic clash of magic and might.

They *must* forget, these humans, these argumentative, greedy, wretched Merchants whose lackeys sprawled across Aerdela, these humans who'd been so pitifully jealous, they'd strung up anyone and everyone with a drop of magic in their veins.

Of course, they didn't call it *magic.*

Folks just had a knack for things. A talent for this, an inclination for that.

And there was a storm brewing.

She could almost see it, in the distance. Inevitably, the lines would tangle, and it'd all come crashing down.

And all the while, the tempest danced on the horizon, ever the reminder of the dying dreams.

Dangerous dreams, more like.

Ada was a dreamer.

That's what the hermit had said, on the shores of the island, as frozen waves had crashed into glittering ice sculptures jutting from the rocky beach, as he'd dragged her to the beyond.

She pressed her eyes closed, fighting back tears.

Even now, Ada's father was preparing his resignation from the Guild Council. Even now, as she paced the bedroom, the Capital knew when she returned the next year, it would not be as a child of the Merchant.

It would be as Commissioner Follerey.

Lilah's letter was burned with regret in Ada's heart.

There would certainly be the tellings.

The rememberings.

And that was where the magic had to stay.

In the distance.

A brewing storm.

Acknowledgements

This story was messy. There are stories that come together with ease and stories are assembled as you swim against the current.

Piecing this together was molasses in winter.

A big thank you to my husband, who has stood by my side through the strangest, most unforeseen storms. This manuscript has been littered with paragraphs of real life, unable to be held back. For all the moments life tossed us against the rocks, he and I have pulled each other up. Thank you, my dear, for having my back, and for helping me pick up the wreckage of this manuscript—this life—and make it beautiful.

Thanks to Lauren, my best friend, for being here while I brought these characters to life, and for struggling through it all together. You are a wonderfully wise mermaid, and the ice isn't forever.

Thank you to Jasmine, for nerding out with me endlessly about our universes, for sharing your beautiful characters with me, and for calling me your brother.

Thanks to Emily, for bringing my characters to life on the metaphorical canvas—it makes my heart sing, truly.

And of course, thank you to everyone who took the time to read this book. I am so grateful to you for taking the plunge with me, and I cannot wait to share the next adventure with you.

C.H. Williams is a queer author, scholar, and occasional musician living in a vaguely coastal region out East. When not causing trouble or spending time with his husband, C.H. Williams can often be found playing with the dog, scribbling away on the next new project, or zoning out to some tunes whilst enjoying nature.